PRAISE FOR T

"This series is exciting, engaging, and got our family to ponder deeper the stories we have read over and over again."

—Cassie Deputies, homeschooling mother of 7

"This series met my expectations precisely. It was exactly what you would expect it to be: a Christian book that was clean and presented biblical history for my newly reading children. I liked most the intertwining of God into things we do and to look to Him for encouragement. This message was loud and clear throughout the pages of the book."

—Wendi Kitsteiner, homeschooling mother

"Imagine is a wonderful, imaginative, Bible-based, historical fiction series that is great for family reading or for individual reading for kids up to about twelve years old. It is full of great lessons in trials and faith. You really can't go wrong adding this to your library!"

—Sabrina Scheerer, homeschooling mother

"I felt the author did a great job pulling the reader into the story. I felt like I was actually in the story."

—Patti Pierce, author of *Truth and Grace Homeschool Academy* blog

". . .a fun read which kept us turning pages, imagining what it may have been like during Noah's time and remembering that things change, but God doesn't, and we should always be thankful. I would definitely recommend the story to those looking for clean reading for kids and biblical fiction!"

–Martianne Stanger, author of
Training Happy Hearts blog

"This one is a page-turner. Once you start, you won't want to put it down. The writing fills your imagination with vivid imagery. One thing that was fun for us to discuss, after everyone had a turn with the book, was how the [story] aligned with the Bible."

–Crystal Heft, author of *Living Abundantly* blog

". . .a great book and we loved reading it aloud together! I recommend you grabbing a copy for your own family to read!"

–Felicia Mollohan, author of *Homeschool4Life* blog

IMAGINE

The Tower Rising

Matt
Koceich

BARBOUR BOOKS
An Imprint of Barbour Publishing, Inc.

Cover illustration: Simon Mendez

Published by Barbour Books, an imprint of Barbour Publishing, Inc., 1810 Barbour Drive, Uhrichsville, Ohio 44683, www.barbourbooks.com

Our mission is to inspire the world with the life-changing message of the Bible.

Member of the
Evangelical Christian
Publishers Association

Printed in the United States of America.

000512 1020 BP

THOUSANDS OF YEARS AGO

The massive tower was now her prison. Its heavy stone walls rose up around her, making any chance of escape impossible. Still, she had run as fast as her young legs could move, hoping to find a way to stop the evil army from reaching heaven. She had put up a good fight to get this far, but it wasn't good enough. She had run straight into a dead end, and the hideous wolf blocked her only way out. The finish line of life was just ahead, covered in mangy fur and sharp fangs. Death was going to greet Bella through the teeth of a wolf.

She was so high up in the air it felt like she was standing at the entrance to heaven. The spiral walkway she had used to ascend the tower with Zion was now empty. Where had all the people gone? Bella hated heights, but to survive the dreaded monster, she had to get over it. The evil one named Gol had already pushed her friend over the edge. . .

She was next.

Her eyes locked on the honey-colored wolf eyes that were locked on her. She could see evil swirling in those yellow orbs like a sulfurous potion brewed in cauldrons of darkest night. The predator inched closer. Five more evil hounds ran up and took their positions behind the alpha. All six were about to tear Bella into a pile of human confetti.

The animals started their chorus of deep, slow growls.

All she could do was stand her ground.

And pray.

Dear God, help me!

CHAPTER ONE

PRESENT DAY

CHICAGO, ILLINOIS

The Windy City was a magical wonderland of glittering lights and sounds. Everywhere she looked, twelve-year-old Bella Rhodes was mesmerized by the epic winter landscape. Store windows trimmed in perimeters of fake snow revealed magical Christmas scenes. Tiny plastic trees were covered with multi-colored ornaments and silver and gold garland. Jolly, life-size Santas and jumbo candy canes filled doorways. Reindeer and elves and gingerbread houses dotted the shelves and display cases.

Her parents had taken Bella and her little sister Eva on a special vacation to celebrate her dad getting a promotion at work. Bella wasn't really sure exactly what her dad did at the bank, but if it could pay for all of them to be in this awesome place, that's all that mattered.

"Who wants hot chocolate?" Bella's dad stopped in front of a Peet's Coffee & Tea.

"Me!" Eva grinned.

"Me too!" Bella added.

The girls followed their parents into a cool little shop where the brewed coffee smelled so good. Bella loved going into Starbucks back home in San Diego. It was like stepping into a novel. All the people lost in their own worlds doing different things. Some filled chairs around the tables and the stools at the bar. Other morning commuters and students sipped their caffeine concoctions in between snippets of conversations.

Bella saw a lady sitting at a tiny wooden table, hands moving across the black keyboard of a silver laptop. The sight made her feel like she was back home. Bella had her mother's old laptop and used it to write stories. And she had a small round table that the laptop sat on too.

Her dad's voice interrupted her musings. "Cake pops?"

Eva shouted, "YES!"

Bella jumped. "Calm down, Eva. You scared me half to death."

Eva ignored her big sister and pointed to the bakery case. "I WANT THE PINK ONE!"

"Bella," her dad said, "let me guess. You want the chocolate one."

"Yes, please."

While her parents ordered the drinks and cake pops, Bella found the only empty table in the house and sat down. The laptop lady was right behind her. Eva stayed with her parents at the counter.

"God understands what you're going through. He knows that deep down you're sad because you don't have a real friend. At least not a friend who loves Jesus and can help you remember truth when you're down."

What on earth?

How does this stranger know how I feel?

She turned around and looked at the lady. But the lady wasn't talking to Bella. She was on her phone.

"You're a child of God, whether you feel like it or not!"

Bella shut her eyes. Whoever was on the other end of the line was going through the exact same thing she was.

"Honey, are you okay?" her mom asked. "Sleepy?"

Bella opened her eyes and looked at her mother.

"Uh. . .yes."

"Now that didn't sound too convincing."

"I'm good. Really."

Her mom smiled.

Eva delivered two hot chocolates to Bella and her mom and went back for more. She returned with two more drinks, and Bella's dad arrived with the bag of cake pops.

"Everybody ready for the tower?"

"Yes, Dad," Eva said. "But let's just focus on getting those cake pops passed out."

"Ha, ha. Very funny."

For a while they sat in silence, enjoying the sweet goodness of their drinks and desserts.

When everyone had finished, Bella's dad pushed his chair back and stood. "We'd better hurry or we're going to run out of time."

They hustled through Riverside Plaza until they came to Jackson Boulevard and turned left. Then they went over the bridge and across the Chicago River where the Willis Tower rose over them with its black aluminum and bronze-tinted glass.

Bella and her family found their way to the Skydeck entrance. They patiently waited in line with the other tourists until it was time for the ride up to the top.

After only sixty short seconds, Bella stepped off the elevator and noticed orange, floor-to-ceiling numbers:

1-0-3. The walls were covered with facts about the tower and video touch screens that allowed visitors to learn about different aspects of the construction process and how Willis Tower compared to other skyscrapers around the world.

Eva scampered away from her parents and wiggled her way through the crowd until she found a glass box that extended out past the walls of the building. Bella caught up to her sister and stopped. A nearby sign called it The Ledge. The carpeted floor turned to see-through glass that gave the tourists a direct view of the street a thousand feet below!

Eva smiled. "Come on, Bella! You're not chicken, are you?"

"No." Bella shuffled out to join her sister.

Her parents caught up with them.

One of the men on the observation deck had a Cubs ballcap on and held an expensive-looking camera. His cellphone started ringing. "Hello." A pause. "Oh, hi, Josephine."

Bella noticed that the man was wearing a T-shirt that had HEBREWS 13:2 in block print on it. Underneath the Bible reference was the hashtag: #*entertainingangels*.

Entertaining angels?

"Are you still at the coffee shop?"

Eva grabbed Bella. "Look B. Look at how far up we are!"

"It's crazy!"

The camera man still spoke on the phone. "You're at Peets?"

Bella remembered that's where they were just a little bit ago.

Another pause.

"B." Eva tugged on Bella's arm. "Look, the people are ants."

"I know." Bella's legs wobbled. Heights were not her thing. She grabbed Eva with both hands.

The camera man looked at Bella. Still speaking into the phone, he said, "Open her eyes."

Bella's legs wobbled more and more, and her head started swimming. She felt like she was going to fall over, so she dropped down right on the floor.

"Bella, what's wrong?"

Bella wasn't sure if it was her mom or dad who asked the question. The Ledge grew blurry. The camera man knelt beside her. She tried to focus on a red car that was stopped at an intersection all the way down on the street. But her eyes wouldn't cooperate.

One more blink of her eyes, and Chicago disappeared.

Bella couldn't believe what had taken its place.

CHAPTER TWO

2300 B.C.

SHINAR

Chicago and all its winter spectacles had simply disappeared.

The observation deck.

Willis Tower.

Her family.

Where am I?

What happened to Mom and Dad? And Eva?

Bella turned in circles looking for her family. How could they have just vanished? How could an entire building be erased from beneath her? And how on earth could she be transported to some unfamiliar world?

God, please help me!

What Bella saw took a while for her brain to process. There were many things that were the same as home.

Grass. Humans. Palm trees. Sunshine. A cool breeze and a bright blue sky. But then, there was a ton of stuff that was very different.

No cars. No stores. No roads or lights. The men wore light-weight skirts tied at the waist with rope. No shirts. The women had on the same skirts as the men, but they wore sheets wrapped like shawls for tops.

The field she was standing in stretched out to the horizon. There were so many people. Bella felt like she'd been dropped into a disturbed ant pile. A flurry of humans scurrying here and there. She turned where she stood to try and see if there was anyone staring at her. She could ask them where she was and where Chicago went.

None of the people looked at Bella and most of them walked by like she wasn't there.

What has happened to me?

Bella looked past the swarm of people and noticed a massive structure rising above the land. From where she stood, it appeared to be a sky-high rocket that rested on one of those gigantic NASA crawler-transport vehicles used to move the old space shuttles from the Vehicle Assembly Building out to the launch complex. She only knew this because her favorite teacher, Mr. Vasquez, was a lover of all things space and wanted to be an aerospace engineer before he became a teacher.

With no idea how to get back to Chicago, Bella improvised.

She started asking for help.

"Excuse me. Do you know how I can get to Chicago?"

Everyone she asked looked at her like she was nuts. None of them answered.

Bella walked up to another group of strangers.

"Sorry to bother you, but I'm trying to get back home."

A young man with dark brown skin smiled at her. "Where is home?"

"You understand me?"

"Of course I do. All of us—all the people you see and the thousands you don't—speak one language."

Bella laughed. "Sorry. Have you heard of a place called Chicago? I'm trying to get back there."

The man shook his head. "No. What's wrong? You don't dress like we do. Where do you live?"

"Chicago. I mean San Diego."

"I don't understand. Which one is it?"

Bella took a deep breath. Her nerves were starting

to get the best of her. "We live in San Diego, California, but my family and I went to Chicago for Christmas vacation."

The young man frowned. "Christmas? Vacation?" He shook his head. "I don't know what you're talking about."

"Where am I?"

"Shinar."

Bella never heard of it. "Okay, thank you."

She moved on to the next group of people, but unfortunately had the same bad luck. No one in this strange place knew how she could get back home.

I'm going to go way out there to that tower-looking thing that looks like it touches heaven. Hopefully someone there will know how to help me.

Bella walked through the crowds for what felt like forever. The more she walked, the bigger the building got. The part that looked like a rocket was actually a tower.

There was never a part of her journey where there weren't people. It was like the whole world lived in this one spot.

At some point, a beautiful river appeared. Its dark blue water sparkled like an invisible giant had sprinkled an endless supply of sun-filled diamonds across the surface. It was getting warm now, and Bella was tempted to jump into the river with her clothes on. She wanted to reach the tower though, so she quickly voted against it.

Bella kept navigating the sea of humanity until she reached a high wall. It surrounded a sprawling city with the pyramid-type structure in the middle. She looked for a way in and found an open gate.

Like her whole time in this alternate place, there were tons of people everywhere in the city. It reminded her of passing period at school. The hallways of Marcus Jones Intermediate turned into a swarm of chaos as kids rushed to get to their next class. Everyone bumped into each other, not thinking about anything except getting to where they were going before the bell rang. They moved in pairs, friends laughing and yelling and talking. Bella would be caught in the middle of it all, kids all around her, all by herself, wondering if anyone ever noticed her.

Here in this *other world* Bella felt the exact same things she felt back home. Lost in the faces.

How would she ever feel like who she was mattered?

Standing inside the gate, Bella felt a seed of panic get planted deep into her heart. As if her question came to life, she looked up and noticed a group of huge men, each holding a cane, staring at her. Bella broke eye contact and started moving away from them. She looked back and noticed they were headed in her direction.

Rushing blood in her veins watered the seed of panic and made it sprout into a full-blown attack. She spun around, telling herself that everything was going to be okay, even though she knew that wasn't true.

"Bella, over here!"

What?

The panic attack blossomed into a gigantic tree of fear.

How does someone in this place know my name?

"Bella?"

She was afraid to find the voice's owner. It was a woman who called her name. And even though the voice sounded sweet and inviting, Bella was too freaked out to answer.

A hand touched her shoulder and she froze. It was like those horror movies where the bad guy slips in behind the victim and reaches out to. . .

"Bella?" Bella turned and saw a face that seemed motherly and warm. Safe. "My name is Evangeline."

More and more people hustled by. Some silent. Others talked about things Bella didn't understand. But in the midst of all the blurry chatter, Evangeline's voice pulled Bella's heart away from the fear that was brewing like a tempest in her soul.

"We've been waiting for you, Bella!"

With this strange lady who didn't make her feel invisible or defensive, Bella wanted to talk.

"How do you know me?"

"Bella," Evangeline said, "in this place you have to have faith. A lot of faith. Many things won't make sense at first, but after time has passed, you will understand."

"Where am I?"

"This is the tower of Babel."

CHAPTER THREE

Bella gazed at the massive city that spread out all around her. For the first time since she arrived here, she wasn't completely freaked out about missing her family. She wasn't thinking about how to get home. She wasn't worried about YouTube, the source of her current joy, or the subscribers she'd never met but whose positive comments were the only bright spots in her day.

Well, maybe she still thought about YouTube. Bella couldn't let it go that easy. Her writing instruction videos were pretty much the only place she felt she got any approval, and it felt good. Her English Lit teacher had noticed Bella's passion for making up stories and suggested she create the videos as a way to encourage kids who didn't like writing.

The videos took off, and Bella had kids from all over

the country thanking her for what she was doing. It felt good to get that kind of attention.

The tower rose above her, higher than even the Willis Tower. Bella was going to make it all the way to the top. How many kids her age got to experience an actual Bible story? She'd guess none.

"Babel?"

"Yes, child. Now, I want you to go and meet my friend Zion." Evangeline pointed her in the direction of a covered doorway. "He will show you the way."

Bella noticed a boy around her age waving at her from the doorway. He was tall and lanky with a head full of thick, curly black hair. His friendly smile made Bella feel a little less nervous about being in this strange place. She headed in his direction.

"Hello! I'm Zion." The boy offered a hand.

"Hi, Zion. My name's Bella." She shook his hand.

The boy looked at her from head to toe. "You are not from around here, are you?"

Bella chuckled. "No. I'm from Chicago, I mean San Diego. But my family is in Chicago."

Zion smiled again. "I haven't heard of those places, but I'm glad you're here with us. This is our city. The people here want to make a name for themselves."

Bella thought she remembered reading that line in her Bible.

The boy led Bella through a series of winding alleyways until they arrived at the base of the tower. "I've heard many stories of a great flood that covered the world. The leaders of this city came up with the tower as a way for the people to reach heaven and become famous. Come on!"

Zion led Bella through a low entry into the base of the tower.

"But Zion, God promised never to flood the earth again. He even gave us the rainbow as a sign of His promise."

Zion shrugged. "People want to make something they can be proud of. Instead of roaming around the land, they choose to stay here. They don't want to be scattered all over the place, so they built this."

Bella followed Zion through a handful of doors and rooms. There wasn't a lot of light, but they managed to keep moving without slowing. Bella walked next to Zion for such a long time her legs hurt.

Eventually, they made it to a narrow walkway on the outside of the tower. She was amazed at the colossal size of the complex. If she had to guess, they were about a hundred levels up now. Looking back down, she saw that the base they had come up through had to be at least ten stories high. Even the dwellings that made up the ancient city looked tiny.

Even up here, people swarmed everywhere. Like worker bees, most of them carried bricks up the walkway to some higher level. The ones who weren't toting bricks hauled large buckets of a dark, gloopy liquid.

"The buckets hold tar," Zion said. "The tar keeps the bricks together."

Bella couldn't believe the number of human beings in one area. It felt like she was back in Chicago looking down from Willis Tower. Thousands of years didn't change human behavior.

Bella watched Zion reach into an object that looked like a huge clay flower pot. Except there was nothing in it. The pot sat close to the tower and seemed to turn a beautiful aquamarine color when Zion reached his hand in. He withdrew a small rope.

"Here, Bella. Put this on. . .around your waist."

Bella took the rope and threaded it through the belt loops on her jeans. There was enough left over for her to tie a knot. This was odd, but she went along with Zion's request.

"Sit down for second."

Bella hesitated. "I thought you were going to take me to the top." She pointed up to the big blue sky.

"I will," Zion said. "But it's better if you sit down while you get used to the belt."

Bella shrugged as she sat down with her back against the tower.

Zion reached into the brilliant blue pot again. He pulled out a small stone.

"Bella, my new friend. Take this and hold it in your hands."

Bella took the rock and noticed writing on it.

PS23

The rope belt vibrated. It made a faint crackling sound, like when her mom dropped a piece of raw chicken in a hot pan of olive oil. The stone felt warm. It softened. The belt still vibrated and crackled. The stone was melting in her hand into a pool of words. . .

My shepherd.

Green pastures.

Calm water.

New strength.

Leads me.

Bella held her hands open as the words swirled

around and around. She looked at Zion. "This is Psalm twenty-three! How is this happening?"

"There's more. Wait." As he spoke to her, Zion was approached by a tall man carrying a cane.

Bella waited. She looked back down at her hands.

Dark valley.

No evil.

With me.

"I'll be right back." It was Zion. Bella looked up and saw him follow the man with the walking stick. The two disappeared around the turn of the walkway. Seconds later a pack of mangy dogs came loping up the path from the lower part of the tower. They stopped in front of her. More kept coming up the path. When they stopped coming, Bella counted twenty dogs in all.

Angry barking commenced. Sharp white fangs were revealed in gaping mouths.

Bella dropped the words and melted stone. But the words didn't fall. Instead, they swirled around her body as the animals inched closer.

Bella watched the random phrases come together to make the complete first verse of the popular Psalm.

The Lord is my shepherd, I lack nothing.

To her left, a very bright light shone. It radiated out

from the shape of a man dressed in layered robes. Bella's eyes couldn't make out specific details of the man's appearance, but it seemed like he had long hair and a very thick beard. He walked through the pack and held out his hand for Bella.

She took it and felt electric. . .alive. . .loved!

Getting to her feet, Bella tried to focus on the man, but the light was too bright. It didn't matter though. At that moment, Bella felt complete. There was no desire she wanted except to keep holding on to the man.

"Come, follow me."

Bella obeyed. The man made a way through the pack of hungry animals and led her to a beautiful place. Even though she had been quite a way up the tower, the walkway she'd been on suddenly stretched out straight, away from the tower, as far as she could see and was no longer crushed rock and dirt but a glorious green blanket of the softest grass.

After some time walking through the beautifully peaceful setting, the man drenched in bright light turned to Bella. "Rest, child."

He pointed to the ground, and Bella sat on the grass. She felt free of any doubt or worry. Safe. After a while, she felt herself getting sleepy. She lay back and looked up at the tower. Soon, the tower became blurry, and the bustle of human activity faded away. Bella slept for what felt like a very long time.

Except, when she opened her eyes, the wild dogs were still there, all huddled together inching their way toward her. Only a stream of water blocked them from reaching her. They growled and barked. One of the dogs stepped into the water but was quickly washed away by the strong current. The remaining pack stayed put on the tower side of the river.

Bella felt strong and confident. She was surprised, because normally fear would have taken over in a situation like the one she was currently in. She remembered jogging with her mom in their neighborhood last week, and a dog ran out at them from a nearby yard. Bella thought she was going to die. The dog barked and ran right up behind her. She could feel the animal's warm breath on the back of her legs.

Bella's prayer life increased exponentially.

She started running as fast as she could, and the dog eventually lost interest and ran back to its yard.

Bella saw Zion back out on the walkway, behind the wild dogs. She felt completely refreshed and was ready to rejoin her new friend. The light form returned. Bella noticed the man held a thick stick in his right hand. He led Bella through the river, and even though the current was strong and she got soaking wet, it did not affect them like it had the dog.

The man bathed in light led Bella safely past the wicked dogs to the walkway where Zion was waiting.

"My love is always with you, child. Be brave."

Bella started to thank the man, but just like that, he disappeared.

CHAPTER FOUR

"Did you see any of that?"

Zion look at Bella, confused. "See what?"

"Those dogs," Bella said pointing, "cornered me over there."

"No, I didn't. Sorry." Zion looked over his shoulder at a man walking farther along up the tower's path. "Sebi needed my help."

Bella shrugged. "Have you worn this belt?" She pulled on the rope Zion had given her.

"Yes, I have my own." He showed Bella his rope belt.

"Is it magic?"

"No," Zion said.

Bella rubbed her hands across her belt. "How did that happen? The man in light looked like Jesus!" Zion smiled.

A strong wind blew over them.

"How?"

"Bella, my new friend. There's more than the belt. Come on, let me show you."

Still awestruck from the experience with the man shrouded in light, Bella didn't push for answers to her question.

The tower path led Bella higher and higher. She guessed they were only about a quarter of the way to the top. Looking over the edge, a wonderful sight spread itself across the landscape below. White birds, elegant doves, perhaps. The delicate creatures flew in a wide circle around the base of the tower. The villagers down on the ground stopped what they were doing and made a human chain around the tower by linking hands.

"Zion, wait!"

The boy stopped. "You okay?"

"Yes, but what's going on down there?"

Zion inched his way to the edge and looked over. "They are thanking the gods for favor in the building of this tower. The stories handed down say that Noah saw a dove when the ark landed. You know, a sign of peace."

Bella considered Zion's words and the two circles of birds and humans. "God, not *gods*, saved Noah."

"The people here in Shinar find their identity in each

other. When they make that circle, they experience a sense of unity." Zion finished his lesson and continued on his way up the tower path.

"But that's wrong! People can't find their identity in—" Bella stopped, thinking about how she too found her identity in others. If she was honest, the people who subscribed to her writing channel on YouTube were like mini gods that made her feel important every time they "liked" one of her posts. Each subscriber made Bella feel a little more fulfilled. A little more complete.

God saved Noah, not gods.

As she continued climbing the tower, Bella's brain made a crazy connection. These people were making an idol with this construction project. They worshipped only what they could see and create with their own hands instead of what they couldn't see and who created them.

God, please help me!

She saw Zion slip into an opening in the tower. Bella hurried behind him, but when she reached the opening and walked inside, she couldn't find her friend.

"Zion?"

A maze of stone rooms and hallways filled the tower's interior. Bella turned in a circle and eventually spotted Zion climbing a set of stone steps that had been built into the tower wall.

"Zion!"

Bella hurried down the halls until she reached the stairs. She navigated the steps two at a time.

Zion slipped out of another opening in the tower wall. By the time Bella caught up and made her way back out onto the walkway, her friend had disappeared.

"Watch out!"

Bella didn't recognize the voice as she was shoved out of the way by a large man carrying a load of bricks.

"Zion!" She called, even though it did no good.

Her mind started racing. What was she doing here? Where was Zion?

She turned and started back down the walkway. Hundreds of people going up gave her impatient looks as they pushed by her. Bella convinced herself that getting down off the tower and finding a way back to Chicago was her best plan. Getting out of Shinar had to happen sooner than later.

But Bella hadn't gone twenty steps before the belt began vibrating around her waist. It crackled and came to life. Bella felt like it was tugging on her, pulling her back in the direction she had come from.

The belt wants me to go back up the tower? I've

officially lost my mind.

She kept walking down the tower path, resisting the urge to turn and go back up. Yes, she was going to miss Zion, but this whole thing was probably a dream anyway.

How could it be a dream? You were standing on the observation deck with your family. Wide awake!

The belt tugged her back, stronger now. The crackling hiss louder than before.

That's when Bella saw the lady named Evangeline. She was coming up the tower path, holding something small in her hand.

"Bella?"

"Hi."

"Are you leaving already? You were brought here for a reason."

Bella gave a quick recap of what had happened on the tower since the last time she had seen Evangeline. "It's not safe for me here. I really need to find a way to get back home."

"Sweet child, let me teach you something more about faith. Here, hold this for a minute." Evangeline handed her the small object she had been holding. It was a small stone. Just like the one Zion had pulled out of the bright blue vessel, this one also had writing on it.

PR16:9

The rope belt vibrated once more. It crackled some more staccato beats. The stone felt warm. . .warmer than the other. After a few seconds passed, it too softened as the other had done, into a puddle of new words. . .

The mind.

Plans.

Way.

The Lord.

Directs.

Steps.

Like the first time, Bella kept her hands open and watched the words swirl. She was not familiar with this verse, but from the letters it had to be from the book of Proverbs.

Bella waited. She looked back down at her hands.

The brilliant light returned, but not covering the beautiful man. This time, the light covered the ground.

As Bella turned and started back up the path of light, she felt that wonderful electric-alive-loved sensation!

Evangeline pointed at the glowing path.

"Dear child, Proverbs 16:9 says, 'In their hearts humans plan their course, but the Lord establishes their steps.'"

At that moment, like before, Bella felt complete. She didn't have that desire to leave.

Follow me.

Bella headed back up the tower path. It didn't matter that she didn't have all the answers. Her heart told her that she was still needed here.

CHAPTER FIVE

Bella followed the path up and around the outside of the tower. She couldn't see Zion, but she felt better about being in this strange place. After experiencing the Bible verses, she was overwhelmed with the feeling that she was here for a reason.

The light on the path started to fade. Still, with no sign of Zion, Bella decided to keep heading up the tower. She was starting to understand how her faith in God was really supposed to work.

Two things were becoming crystal clear. First, she didn't need another person to make her feel worthy. She was enough because God was with her.

It doesn't matter if no one subscribes to my channel. I am someone because God loves me.

The second thing Bella was understanding about how real faith worked was that God does care and He leads His children. Even if the situation seems crazy odd, God is still there.

More waves of people swept past in both directions. Most of the men who headed up the path carried the stones or buckets of tar. The women Bella saw carried everything from big clay jars and armfuls of fruit to babies wrapped in cream-colored linens. Children of all shapes and sizes zigzagged through the grown-ups as they ran about doing who knew what.

As Bella tried taking in all the sights, another one of the wild dogs appeared. It came up from behind her and stayed on her right side. It didn't turn on her like the others had. The dog just trotted up the path next to Bella.

She noticed that the animal's paws were really big. And its head and jaws seemed bigger than other dogs its size that she'd seen. Maybe she was just imagining it, but when the dog turned to look back at Bella, its eyes were yellow.

A pair of hands grabbed Bella by the shoulders.

She craned her head back and saw Evangeline's beautiful smile.

"You scared me," Bella said.

"Sorry, but I saw that wolf getting close to you."

"Wolf?"

"Yes, that guy and all his furry buddies are wolves, not dogs. They all belong to Gol and his people. Don't mess with them and you'll be okay."

"Who's Gol?"

Evangeline let go of Bella's shoulders. "He's the man in charge of building this thing." She spread her arms out to indicate the tower.

Bella watched the wolf get lost in the crowd.

"Why does he need wolves to build a tower?"

"That," said Evangeline, "is the mystery. Gol is a man who leads these people to do this thing that they would not do on their own. Everyone looks up to him like he's their savior."

"That's kinda weird."

"Yes, it is weird."

The two walked up the tower path in silence for quite some time. When they reached a level that had a barricade, Evangeline grabbed Bella's shoulders again.

"I'm not allowed to go any farther. Be strong, child."

"Why can't you come with me?"

"Don't worry about that now. Just go, and be brave." Like the wolf only moments before, Evangeline walked away and disappeared into the mass of people heading back down the tower path.

Bella took a deep breath and exhaled.

God, thank You for leading me.

She looked out over the edge to the city far below. The higher she climbed, the more magical this ancient world became. Did these people actually think they could build the tower to reach heaven? How would that work? It wasn't like there was a sign with the word HEAVEN on it floating in the clouds.

Hoping to find Zion, and having no idea where he could be, Bella ducked into a passageway that took her back inside the tower. Flicks of shadow rushed past her eyes, like tiny blackbirds zooming by in search of a hidden perch. There was nothing near her that would create those darting shadows. It was odd, but it certainly wasn't the first odd thing to happen since she had arrived in Shinar.

Bella stepped into a small room that was connected to the main hall. Inside, she found it empty except for a pile of stones that had been left in the middle of the floor. More black spots filled her vision. Her brain was tired from all the input, but she had to push on and get to the top of the tower. She noticed a small doorway on the opposite side of the room. Bella went through it and found herself in another room, also with a pile of stones in the center of the floor. There were no more doors or passageways, so Bella turned to leave. That's when she saw a piece of paper sticking out from the stone pile. She pulled it out and found that it was a scroll with writing on it. It also had a sketch of the tower with the city complex at its base.

Together we will reach heaven.
Together we will become famous.
Together we will not be scattered.

"That doesn't belong to you."

Bella dropped the scroll. When she looked to see who was there, she saw a wolf. She said a prayer and bent down to retrieve the scroll. When she stood, Bella saw a man standing behind the wolf. He was tall and wore a robe that showed off his muscles. Mean-looking. Intimidating.

Don't be afraid.

"Who does own it?"

"Gol."

Bella held on to the scroll. She stood tall and looked the man in the eyes. "Do you know who I am?"

"I don't care who you are. You don't belong here, and you need to leave."

"I need to see Gol," Bella said. "I need to tell him something."

The man squinted at her, like a clerk checking to see if a customer's bill is counterfeit. "Who are you?"

"My name is Bella Rhodes."

I am a child of God and you can't do anything to me.

After an awkward silence, a young person slipped in the room behind the tall man.

"Abimah! That's my friend. She's nice."

Bella couldn't believe it.

"Zion!"

CHAPTER SIX

"Bella!"

The friends hugged, but not before the man with the weird name took the scroll away. "You won't need this."

Zion grabbed Bella's hand. "Come on. Don't worry about that. It's just a piece of paper."

"But why does that man want it? Why is that paper so important?"

Zion led Bella back out to the walkway. The sun seemed dimmer. Not as many people were trudging along in either direction. Heavy clouds, darkening from their watery burdens, filled the ancient sky.

"It was just a motto the leaders wrote on parchment and passed out to whoever would take it." Zion talked as he made his way up the tower path, kicking rocks as he went.

"Why did that man get so upset?" Bella picked up

her pace and caught up with Zion. "It was like I was robbing him of some prized possession."

"Abimah is an old friend of our family. He was one of Gol's first helpers on this tower. He was the one who thought up the motto. Gol accepted his motto as a personal thank-you for his willingness to serve."

Bella didn't get why the guy would be so edgy about the paper, but then she was reminded of how edgy she got every time she checked her social media accounts. If she read a positive comment or got a new "like," the world was a great place to be. If no one subscribed or liked her online presence, then the world was gray and sad.

They kept climbing up the tower walkway, Bella still amazed at how people without modern machines could create something so epic.

After a while, the number of people dwindled to only a fraction of what it had been. Just a few men and women passed in either direction. None of them made eye contact with Bella. They went on their way without even offering a wave or a head nod. The people's personalities seemed to change the higher up Bella went.

As she rounded the edge of the tower, Bella counted five big men standing on the path, acting as human roadblocks. In front of each man stood a wolf. The animals' tongues were hanging out, like they had been running and were now trying to cool off and catch their breath.

"Gol's men. Come on." Zion pulled Bella off the path and directed her to another opening in the tower. Just inside the shadowy entryway, Bella saw another pot like the one Zion had pulled the rope belt out of earlier.

She watched him reach into the ceramic pot and pull out a silver T-shirt. "Put this on."

Nothing was normal in this place, but Bella remembered how awesome it felt to experience God's word after putting the belt on. She quickly slid the silver shirt on and waited for something magical to happen.

Nothing.

"Hey, Zion. What's going on?"

Zion looked back out at the men guarding the path. "Every once in a while, Gol has men blocking the path. There've been people who try to stop the tower from being built. They don't think it's right. Some even say it goes against what God commanded."

Bella couldn't agree more. Those people were exactly right. "God told Noah and his family to multiply and fill the earth. Putting all of this time and energy into building a tower keeps them from obeying God."

"How do you know these things?" Zion asked.

"I read my Bible."

Zion frowned at her. "I don't know anything about that, but maybe you need to go out there and tell the guards what you just told me."

"I'm just a kid, but I've got God on my side!"

Zion shook his head. "That's right, Bella. I don't care if you're two or two hundred. You're here. You believe God has a reason for you being here. And if that reason is to confront Gol and have him stop building, then we need to get by the guards."

Still nothing crazy happened with the silver shirt. No vibrations. No glowing lights or Bible verses that came to life.

One of the men blocking the way made eye contact with Bella. Despite his intimidating build, Bella used this as a chance to connect with him.

"Are you going to let us pass?" she asked.

"No," the man said gruffly. "You and your little friend here need to go back down to whatever hole you live in."

Now the shirt moved. Just a bit, but Bella felt it. Like a flag rippling in a soft breeze.

"God's got this!"

The man looked at her like she was wearing a clown suit. "What?"

Bella felt the rope belt now. It vibrated like before.

"I said, God's got this."

The man laughed. "His name is *Gol*, with an *L*. Seriously, go home."

Zion started to say something, but Bella cut him off.

"I need to see Gol. I need to tell him that building this tower is a mistake."

Another laugh and smirk. "If you think a little girl is going to be the reason this tower doesn't get finished, you're out of your mind."

The disrespectful brute hadn't finished his sentence before an imposing figure who wore a heavy dark cloak walked up to the line of men and wolves. A hood covered its face. Both guards and wolves backed up and bowed. They stayed in that position until the figure passed, then reformed their line.

"Sir, this girl believes she has something important to say to you."

"Is. That. So?" The voice was deep and mechanical, like Darth Vader. Each word was spoken like it was a complete thought.

"Yes, sir." The guard's words irritated Bella, but she

maintained her composure. "She claims that you should stop building the tower."

All the guards laughed. The wolves started howling as if they thought it was funny too.

But the newcomer didn't make a sound. A gaunt hand came from the folds of the robe and pulled back the hood. A man who looked more wraithlike than human stared at Bella with eyes the color of coal.

Who has black eyes?

A tremor of energy ruffled across her new shirt. Bella knew that, given the situation and the thing that was standing across from her, she should be on the verge of full-blown terror. But the silver shirt Zion had her put on seemed to help her stay strong.

"Child, is this true?"

Another flow of power coursed over Bella. Her brain finally brought her up to speed. The man-thing in front of her had to be Gol.

"Yes." *You've got this, Bella Rhodes. You've got this!*

She sometimes found "self-talk" to be rather helpful in situations like the one she was currently in.

"May I ask," Gol said slowly, "who says I should stop?"

This is your chance to stand up for God. Not that He needs you to, but what an honor...

"God says."

"God?"

Out of the corner of her eye, Bella could tell the guards were still snickering. The wolves had stopped howling, although each one kept their eyes glued to her.

"Yes, God."

Gol considered her answer. "You and God are friends?"

"Yes. And I'm here to tell you that He told Noah to fill the earth. This tower. . .this city. . .all the people are in one place. You aren't doing what He said."

Gol nodded. He didn't say anything more.

Instead, he turned and motioned to one of the guards. The darkly wrapped figure pointed at Bella and then up at the sky.

The guard who had been talking to her patted the wolf in front of him. The wild animal stood and started to move in Bella's direction.

Her new shirt pulsed.

She stood her ground.

The wolf leaped.

CHAPTER SEVEN

Bella jumped back and used her arms to knock the wolf's jaw away. It snapped angrily as it went away from its target.

The guard also lunged at Bella, decreasing her odds of getting away.

She jumped back again. The tower was behind her. There was an opening the size of a window. That was her escape route.

Zion threw a rock at the guard, distracting him long enough for Bella to get through the opening. The wolf jumped in right after her.

Fast as lightning, Zion jumped in after the wolf.

As the wild creature pounced at Bella a second time, Zion tackled it from the side. Both wolf and boy landed against the tower wall with a thud.

"Lyaar, stop! The girl means no harm. Return to Gol."

The wolf moved its head back and forth between Zion and Bella, like it actually understood what the boy had said.

"Return," Zion repeated.

The wolf snapped in Bella's direction, but then jumped back through the opening and disappeared.

"What just happened?"

Zion stood and took Bella's hand. "Come on. We need to hurry."

"You can talk to wolves?"

Zion led Bella through a maze of rooms and hallways. At some point, they found a stone stairway that led up into the darkness. "In a way, I guess. I've been around them since they were pups. I have a special connection with Lyaar. All the other wolves have no problem enforcing Gol's wishes. Lyaar, on the other hand, seems to question her master's motives at times."

Bella followed Zion up the stairs.

"How do you know which one that is? All the wolves look the same to me."

Zion stopped climbing and looked at Bella. "Lyaar has a small patch of white fur on her back left leg."

Each step of the way brought Bella more questions than answers.

A group of people, a man and two women, made their way down the stairs. As they passed, one of the women bumped Bella and kept going. The other woman also bumped into her. The man looked at Bella and scowled at her. He said, "Watch where you're going."

The three strangers disappeared down the stairs.

"Man, talk about rude."

Zion resumed climbing the stairs and Bella followed.

"For some reason, the higher up you go in the tower, the more impatient the people become. Sorry."

"It's not your fault." Bella trudged along, following Zion higher and higher up the tower. The city below faded into blurry outlines of buildings and faint dots of people. She definitely felt like she was way higher now than she had been back in Chicago with her family in Willis Tower.

When they reached the next landing, Zion stopped to rest. Bella was secretly glad for the break because the higher up they went, the harder it was to breathe.

After a quick break, the two made their way to the outer walkway. Bella wondered where Gol and his guards had gone. Her attention from following Zion was now diverted to the sky. A mixture of dark clouds and rainbows swirled together in the oddest sight

Bella had ever seen.

The temperature dropped. The air picked up speed and made it even harder to breathe.

But breathing soon became a secondary matter, because the world around the tower changed. And the change wasn't something fun like balloons and butterflies raining down from the sky. No, the change was powerful and intimidating.

The sky illuminated in a brilliant explosion of golds and lemons. Shades of orange and red. Forceful winds kept blowing against the tower, threatening to knock Bella off her feet. She sat down and held on to a heavy boulder that was next to her for support.

Bella saw a figure of a man appear in the clouds. It looked like he wore a long coat that stopped at his feet and had a belt of gold cinched around his chest. She counted seven gold lights that seemed to float in the air above the man's head. White hair covered his head, and two pools of fire took the place of his eyes. His face was shining like the sun, although it didn't hurt to stare at him.

His feet seemed to be covered in shiny brass.

What on earth am I looking at?

Who *on earth am I looking at?*

As bizarre as the scene was, Bella wasn't afraid. The exact opposite feeling poured over her as she sat there soaking in the vision. This man was the complete opposite of Gol. Where the tower leader was wrapped in darkness, this man was filled with light.

There was no sign of Zion. Maybe he was still close by, but the sky man took all of her attention. Bella felt like her heart was being filled by a greater love than she'd ever known as she watched more of the heavens open.

As she held on to the boulder, Bella heard the sound of powerful rushing water. It appeared that the man was talking, but she couldn't understand what he was saying. As he spoke, he held out his right hand to reveal seven brilliant stars. And then a sword came out of the man's mouth as he spoke!

"Bella?"

Was he calling her name?

"Bella, are you okay?"

That's when her brain registered that it was Zion who was talking.

"Zion, where are you?"

"Over here. To your right."

Bella blinked. The incredibly insane vision had

vanished just as quickly as it had appeared. She saw Zion just a few feet away. "Did you see that?"

"Yes! It was amazing!"

Bella pulled herself up. She stretched out a hand and helped Zion get to his feet.

Zion let go of her hand. "What...*who* was that?"

Bella brushed off her jeans. Words escaped her. Her whole body buzzed with excitement. She felt energized to keep heading up the tower. She had to make it to the top. Even though she knew how the Bible story ended, Bella felt like God was letting her be a part of this story. She felt a new connection here. God gave her worth, and she had His approval. She had to trust Him.

"Zion, I have a good idea who it was."

"Who?"

"Come on. I'll tell you as we go."

CHAPTER EIGHT

PRESENT DAY

MINDGATE 2 FACILITY
FLORENCE, OREGON

He loved watching the mighty Pacific Ocean. From the roof, he had a great view of the vast expanse of water. He was getting mentally prepared for his meeting with the Master. Yes, after what happened at the camp in North Carolina, he was going to have to come up with a better plan at keeping their work on the Electus project secret. He couldn't have the enemy getting word of what they were doing, or the whole plan would have to be scrapped.

"Sir?"

The voice belonged to one of his minions, Brad Barron.

The man ignored the newcomer. Maybe he would go away.

"Sir, sorry to interrupt, but I think you'll want to know what's happening."

Yes, he loved the water. Now, in the middle of the day, with the sunlight reflecting across the surface. It was like a watery star field. Diamonds sparkling over the ocean, making his thoughts clear. A gull flew by, distracting him.

"Sir?"

The seabird soared away. Maybe Barron would do the same.

"Sir, it's Marabel Calvert. She says it's important."

Marabel Calvert?

The man turned his icy green eyes away from the ocean and put them directly on his assistant. "What does she want?"

"Just said she has a note for you."

Marabel Calvert was one of only three names that Barron was instructed to entertain. All others were turned away.

"Tell her I'll be down in a few minutes."

Barron bowed like the man was his sensei and quickly vanished into the enormous building.

It made him furious that his quiet time with the ocean had been compromised. He'd have to make it up later. For now, there was a problem he had to take care of.

—

As he made his way through Beryl Sector, passing by gem-encrusted walls that reflected their golden-yellow color, he planned his course of action. This section of the Mindgate facility always made him feel like he was walking through the sun. He knew meeting with Marabel Calvert was the only thing he could do. If he didn't, they would just send one of the other two soldiers.

He took a deep breath and opened the door to the lobby.

"Hello, Ms. Calvert. Barron said you were here to see me."

The old lady opened her purse and fished out a small envelope. She handed it to the man.

"An invitation?"

"Perhaps."

"A bomb?"

Ms. Calvert's lack of emotion said she didn't find the sarcasm the least bit funny.

"What if I don't open it?"

"Then consider yourself warned."

The man raised his eyebrows. "Do I detect a threatening tone, Marabel?"

"No, Konrad. Only a promise."

Konrad opened the envelope and pulled out a piece of paper. He unfolded it. After a few seconds of silence, the lady spoke.

"Well?"

"You can't be serious."

"We are."

Konrad crumpled the paper up and tossed it over his shoulder. "Close all the Mindgate facilities?"

"Yes. All of them."

"Would you do me a favor and come to my office?"

The old lady stepped around Konrad and retrieved the crumpled paper. "Only if it will help you make the right decision."

"Of course, Marabel. Of course."

After a few minutes, the two arrived in Konrad's office located on the far end of Onyx Sector. He opened a floor-to-ceiling glass door and motioned for his guest to enter.

"Please, have a seat."

Ms. Calvert found two brown leather chairs next to the window that looked out onto the Pacific. "Nice view." She waited until Konrad found his seat.

"Yes, the ocean helps." Konrad sat in one of the chairs.

Ms. Calvert sat in the other.

For a few minutes, neither Konrad Lynch nor Marabel Calvert spoke. The only noise was the hum of a small refrigerator motor.

"I give you credit, Marabel. Out of all the representatives they could send, they sent you."

"No, that's where you're wrong. I sent myself."

Konrad pulled his right foot up onto his left knee. "I can't even close this facility, let alone all the others."

"We both know that's not true. You hold a very high level of authority. Eric Ful would not have you in charge if he thought you weren't qualified."

"Point taken. May I ask how you found me?"

Ms. Calvert sat up straight. "One of your employees, Mr. Nah. He worked for a kids' camp out in North Carolina. He was caught trying to connect with two of the campers. He showed them your Electus site and would have done much worse if we hadn't created a diversion."

"Yes, one of your army set fire to the guardhouse. The campers left Nah's cabin, then left the camp."

"Your intel never ceases to amaze me. However, I can't sit here all day. There's a war being waged, and I need to go help."

Konrad put his foot back down. Now it was his turn

to sit up in his chair. He considered the lady in front of him.

"Nah will be dealt with. As far as the facilities closing, I can't help."

"Mr. Lynch, I am going to come back soon. If I find Mindgate still open, all of the facilities will be destroyed."

—

Konrad Lynch watched Marabel Calvert leave the facility. He had no doubt that she meant every word of her *promise*. It was time to contact his people.

Gol. Can you hear me?

Gol, I need you to do whatever it takes to keep the girl from leaving.

Keep the tower rising until you get to heaven.

Don't stop.

The Master wants to raise his throne above the stars of God.

Take it higher than the clouds.

The Master wants to reclaim his rightful place. . .the one he had before being cast down to earth.

Gol, our position has been compromised. Make the Master proud.

We don't have much time.

Have the people work faster. We will send more wolves.

Do not stop building until you see the gates of the city of the enemy!

CHAPTER NINE

2300 B.C.

SHINAR

Gol stood on the edge of the path and looked down on the world far below. He felt his power rising along with the tower he was standing on. The people saw him as supreme ruler. They all believed him when he said the tower would unify them and make them stronger as a community. When a few challenged him with some nonsense about God telling the people to spread out all around the world, he stood firm, and the opposition had finally given up.

"Yes, Konrad. I hear you," Gol said out loud. "If you were here right now, you would be impressed. It is so beautiful. Be assured, I will do all that it takes to keep Bella from leaving."

The girl is not a problem. Meddling Zion is who I am

focusing on. He is giving her pieces of the enemy's armor. Jesus thinks I'm just a madman who has a wolf or two by my side. No, I will make the Master proud.

Gol heard Konrad's voice just as clearly as if Konrad were standing on the tower next to him. He pointed to the sky. "The tower will keep rising until we get to heaven. My men are making bricks and baking them thoroughly. I will order them to work faster. I will order more tar to be brought in to complete the work."

Never stop. Nothing will get in our way. Nothing.

Gol continued, "We will never stop. No child will stop me. The one named Bella doesn't belong here. I don't know how she came, but I will make sure she learns her lesson."

When we get to heaven, we will raise the Master's throne above the stars of the enemy!

Gol smiled. "I can't wait to see the Master's face when he finally steps back into the place from which he fell so long ago. Oh, the faces of those who were not banished. . .I can't wait to see them! Will they be surprised? Shocked? Afraid? Oh, I cannot wait!"

Yes, we will take it higher than the clouds. Higher and higher still!

Gol spread his arms wide. "The view is spectacular. I

am honored to be called to lead our people higher and higher. Even the clouds are almost below us!"

I believe the soldier Daemon has been overseeing Nah and his actions at Oak Bay. I will contact him and make sure he knows what to do. I am confident that he can finish our work there. We don't have much time.

"Yes," Gol said. "I will speed up our project. Don't worry, I promise I won't sacrifice any detail. A perfectly constructed tower that will stand on this wonderful site for time immemorial is what I will complete. I promise to make the people work faster. There will be no rest until the tower is finished."

We will welcome more wolves.

"The beautiful creatures always have a home with me," Gol said. "The more wolves the better."

We will not stop until we reclaim our rightful places.

Gol brought his arms together and interlocked his fingers. "I will not stop until the gates of heaven are right before our eyes."

———

No one who walked by Gol and witnessed him talking to himself would ever call him crazy. No, that would never happen. They would perhaps call him a mastermind. Sometimes masterminds had to talk to themselves to get things done. Besides, anyone who knew Gol knew that he constantly talked to himself. That's what their leader did. Talked to himself and got the tower of Babel built.

But Zion knew better.

He knew that Gol wasn't talking to himself. Zion knew who Gol really was and who he worked for. It was time to help the girl Bella learn about her special calling. She had to know that her reason for being here on the tower was so much more than stopping a madman.

It was time to give her the rest of the armor and prepare for war.

CHAPTER TEN

"We need to hurry. We're not going to get far without problems." Zion picked up speed, jogging up the spiral path. Bella hustled to keep pace.

The sky showed no trace of the brilliant display that had just presented itself. The dark clouds had been pulled in front of the scene like heavy gray stage curtains hiding the action from the eager audience.

As they maneuvered through the workers laden with their buckets of tar and armloads of bricks, Bella called out to Zion, "I think I know what all that crazy stuff we just saw in the sky was."

"Yeah," Zion said without turning around. "You were going to tell me."

"Well, I remember in the Bible, in Revelation, a part where a guy named John has a vision of Jesus. What we just saw is pretty much the same thing that John saw when Jesus appeared to him!"

Zion stopped moving. He turned to face Bella. "It's time for me to tell you that are here for so much more than reaching the top of this tower."

Bella skidded to a stop to keep from plowing into her friend.

She heard what he said, but her brain was trying to process what was happening on the path behind Zion.

Wolves. Many more than before. Tons of the rabid creatures blocked the path. Like a newly disturbed ant pile, the wolves moved every which way over the path. Into each other. Over each other. Under each other. Snapping. Growling. Biting.

Total chaos.

"Zion, behind you!"

Without turning around, her guide could hear what was happening. "Wolves, right?"

"Yeah. Like ants!"

Zion grabbed Bella's hand and tried to pull her into an opening in the tower wall, but more wolves were waiting there.

"There have never been this many!" Zion shouted to be heard over the yelping and manic barking of the wolves.

Bella couldn't figure out where all the wolves were coming from. They poured out of the tower openings, dropping down onto the ones that were already occupying the path. Behind Bella and Zion, the walkway was also loaded with wolves. All the animals inched forward to corner their prey.

Zion reached into one of his pockets and pulled out something that looked like a pair of glowing mittens. "Bella put these on your feet!"

He tossed them to Bella and after she caught them, she realized they weren't mittens, but coverings for her feet.

"They're shoes of peace. From the gospel!"

Bella slipped the coverings on over her sneakers. She took a couple practice steps and heard the ground crunch. The coverings Zion had given her had transformed into cleats.

The wolves came closer and closer.

This time the wild animals were going to be successful.

Even though Bella couldn't see a way out, she closed her eyes and prayed.

Lord, I don't know if this is a dream or not, but it sure feels real. Please help me!

A figure in a dark cloak appeared on the path ahead

of Bella and Zion. It seemed to be floating over the pack of wolves.

The Darth Vader voice came from the figure in the cloak. "This is your last warning. Either work with me or take your last couple of painful breaths."

Bella was surrounded. Zion didn't seem to have any more help to give. They were finally trapped.

"JUMP!" Zion yelled.

His voice was so powerful, the wolves cringed before them.

Bella jumped.

She landed beside Zion on the wolves.

"RUN!"

Bella ran over the tops of the wolves, who had been shocked by the power of Zion's voice. Her spiked shoes gave her traction to push across the animals' backs.

Gol jumped to the side in a flash, making a move to intercept Bella.

She ducked under his arms, landed on the ground, and rolled until she found her feet. Standing, she was now on the other side of Gol and the giant pile of wolves.

Zion was farther up the tower path. "Come on, Bella. Don't stop!"

Somewhere overhead thunder ripped across the

ancient sky. Vengeance from the heavens. Lightning cut its way down in white jagged lines, over and over, in mighty pulses.

A white, hot fiery bolt of lightning shot down and exploded into the brick tower just feet in front of Bella. The intense energy blew a wide hole in the path.

Tons of wolves crumbled with the brick and went over the edge of the hole, falling down into oblivion.

One more step, and Bella would have met the same fate as Gol's furry horde.

Zion stood on the opposite side of the hole. He waved at Bella to move.

"Come on. Jump! The shoes will help you climb!"

Bella turned and saw the wolves inching closer to her. Gol moved with them. She had no choice. She moved back and took a running leap.

Zion had his hands outstretched, but Bella didn't jump far enough. She clung to the side of the hole left by the lightning. She heard Zion yelling above her.

"You got it!"

Bella used the cleats to help her gain traction in the rock and looked for handholds.

She kept climbing and then reached up as far as she could. . .

Her hand touched Zion's.

He pulled her up, out of the pit. Her legs collapsed underneath her, just as they had in Willis Tower on the Skydeck. She suddenly thought of her family. Were they freaking out looking for her? Was this just a crazy dream?

No, it was really happening. The time travel thing still didn't make sense, but maybe it wasn't time travel.

Open her eyes. . .

The guy at Willis Tower. The one with the camera, talking to someone on his phone.

Crazy.

But there wasn't time to figure it all out. For now, she had to warn the people that the tower was really an idol. She wanted to warn them against it going any higher. She needed to help them know that they needed to get their approval from God, not from the things they did or what they accomplished.

Like YouTube. It doesn't matter if no one subscribes. God approves of me!

But there was a whole mess of vicious animals and an evil leader prepared to do whatever it took to stop her.

CHAPTER ELEVEN

Suddenly, it was like the heavens had been cut by some gargantuan, supernatural blade. The sky began to bleed black. Dark bands spread out in all directions until all the world was dim.

In addition to the near darkness, the tower became enshrouded in an eerie, misty fog.

Bella sensed a change in the air. Colder.

"I feel like we're in a horror movie." She shivered from the quick drop in temperature.

Zion kept moving forward up the path. "A what?"

"You know, like a really freaky show that scares everybody."

Zion didn't respond.

Bella sighed. "Never mind. It's just getting scary up here on the tower. The sky looks like it's dying."

The pair kept heading up the winding path.

Bella couldn't help but wonder what Gol's next move would be. She had so little faith in her ability to stop the evil man. She was just a kid, who hadn't accomplished much in her short life.

"Bella, you are strong. Don't stop now."

Zion's voice was smooth and reassuring. The spoken tones resonated in her ears, bringing a calmness over her whole body. She couldn't imagine being here without him.

"Zion, it's getting harder to focus up here."

The words had just left her mouth when Bella was brought up short by a burning spear that whizzed by her face and impaled the path in front of her. She looked up and saw a gaunt shape hanging out of a window several stories above them. Mere seconds passed before a handful of flaming spears rained down around her.

She jumped back and forth, dodging the falling spears.

The burning weapons drove into the dirt path, sending up chunks of dirt in Bella's face.

Zion jumped forward. "Come on, Bella! We've got to go!"

The fire kept coming from somewhere above them. So this was Gol's next move. Commanding his men to throw flaming spears. Was everyone on the tower under Gol's authority? Didn't any of them see that this was a useless endeavor?

One of the spears scraped Bella's arm as she flew down the path. The searing pain caused her to stumble.

"Zion, help!"

"What is it?" He looked over and saw that Bella was holding her arm. He moved close and took hold of her hand. "Come on. We've got this!"

More fiery spears poured down. By mere inches, Bella was spared a very painful experience. One of the spears just missed her head and chest.

The two ran faster up the spiral path, dodging the spears as they went. Zion led Bella to another ceramic vessel that rested against the tower wall. This one was bigger than the both of them. He reached in and pulled out an object that looked like a thin, translucent bath towel. It sparkled with yellow bursts of energy all over its surface.

Zion snapped the thing away from his body and Bella watched it stiffen into a shield.

"Use this and follow me!"

Bella grabbed it and held it over her head. As soon as she did, the spears crashed into the shield and fell, harmless, to the ground. She raced behind Zion, keeping the shield up the whole time.

Zion put on the brakes as they rounded the path. Their way was blocked by more hungry wolves.

Suddenly there were men dropping down onto the path in front and behind Bella and Zion. Every one of them held a flaming shaft of wood in each hand.

One of the men inched forward a few steps. His eyes were black like the sky over them. He held the burning spears up in front of her, and the spears stopped raining down from above.

"Gol, the powerful one, told us to offer you one last chance to join him. If you refuse, we've been commanded to show you no mercy."

Bella's heart skipped a beat. The man's voice was deep and robotic. The fire on the tips of his spears gave off enough heat to sear her face.

Jesus, please help me! I can't do this without You!

Instinctively, she put the shield in front of her. The energy from it coursed through her hands and up her arms. It gave her strength. Courage. Boldness to stand up for what was right.

"I am here to make the people understand that they are not obeying God."

The man thrust one of his spears at Bella's legs. She jumped back.

"Are you ready to join Gol? Yes or no."

Zion pointed up. Bella looked and saw an open window in the tower wall. It was too high for her to reach. What was Zion thinking?

"Yes or no?"

Zion then pointed at his feet.

Feet and the window?

"YES OR NO?"

Her stalling tactic was finished.

Feet and the window. Feet and the window. The cleats!

It all came together in her mind.

"NO!" Bella screamed as she jumped up on the side of the tower wall. She slipped back down to the ground. It was impossible to climb with the shield. Just as she thought that, it went limp—back into the form of a towel. Bella tossed it over her shoulder and jumped back onto the wall. She was able to climb up several feet by grabbing onto bricks like she was at The Wall back home in San Diego, climbing up the man-made rock walls.

Wolves jumped up underneath her, snapping with razor-sharp teeth. Groaning howls let Bella know that they were waiting for her to lose her grip and fall.

Zion had already made it to the window opening.

Just a few more feet and Bella would be there too.

"Use the shield! Open it back up and push it to me."

Bella pulled the towel from around her neck and snapped it out.

She held the shield above her head. She stood up on her toes and stretched. . .

Zion grabbed the shield and pulled Bella through the window just as the wild man's spears slammed into the wall.

CHAPTER TWELVE

It was an unveiling of what was yet to come. A powerful vision of a battle so insane and so epic, words weren't enough.

Bella stood on the banks of a very large, very wide river. The powerful water flowed down through the fertile valley. To her right, a large mountain rose over the beautiful land of patchwork fields and stands of dark green trees.

A figure came down from the sky—a form of light shaped like a human—holding a massive bowl with the word WRATH engraved on its side. The being floated down and hovered over the middle of the river. Bella was not afraid of the supernatural newcomer. The bowl was poured out over the river. Lava-like liquid flowed from the bowl into the water, creating a heavy fog.

The massive river dried up just as fast as the wind blew through the trees. It reminded Bella of a plug being pulled out of a bathtub. Water went down some unseen hole, and after a short while, all that remained was dry land. The river had vanished, leaving no trace that it had ever been there.

Three new figures, each covered in dark robes, appeared out of the fog. These, unlike the one who held the bowl named WRATH, *were very ominous in appearance. Bella found herself inching backwards, farther up the riverbank. The figures were the size of grown men but appeared to have reptilian features. Their skin looked wet and shiny. Almost slippery.*

They wore no coverings on their large, webbed feet. Their eyes were the freakiest part. They were located on either side of the figures' heads and bulged out.

Bella heard croaking sounds.

Like frogs.

She hid behind a boulder and watched the three frog-people take off running. As they passed her, their croaks became intelligible. "Let's go gather all the kings of the world so we may bring them back here and prepare for the Great Battle."

Bella got up from her hiding place and surveyed the land. There were no signs of life. Only the farmland of the valley and the dried-out riverbed.

The air had an acrid tinge now. Like a thousand fires were burning just past the horizon, and the wind carried the fragrance of ash and ember over Bella and the valley.

She couldn't believe what happened next. The valley split in two. A massive earthquake ripped open the land, sending plumes of ash and smoke up into the air.

A dark king rose from the abyss. He climbed out of the fault and stared at her.

"Abaddon!" Unseen voices cried the name out, over and over. After a while, Bella started to think it sounded like they were saying, "A Bad Man. A Bad Man."

She watched as the king with the bizarre name lifted up his strong arms toward the darkening sky. Valley and mountain were completely wrapped in the smoky haze.

From the horizon came kings and their armies from all the nations of the world. They yelled out that they had come to fight the Lord.

Bella felt a shiver run down her spine. This couldn't be. Who would want to fight Jesus? There were so many people armed with every type of weapon known to mankind.

"Abaddon! Destroyer! King of the Abyss!"

Screams from the soldiers filled the air. Evil chants sung in praise to the dark king.

The sun turned dark as the earth's furnace continued to shoot up flame and smoke.

More and more earthly armies arrived and filled every possible section of the valley.

Bella had seen many crazy things up to that point, but now her eyes saw an even crazier scene. Young people appeared, kids her age, both boys and girls, standing in a ring all around the outside of the valley. The ring of children encircled the gathered armies. The children stood battle-ready armed like soldiers with swords and shields, helmets and breastplates...

Standing side-by-side with the children were angels with their horses and chariots of fire.

One of the angels looked at Bella and smiled.

"Are you ready?" the angel asked.

"Yes!" Bella roared.

"Let's go!"

Bella ran.

CHAPTER THIRTEEN

They climbed and climbed all night, slipping past hungry wolves and anxious guards along the way. They did this without saying a word to each other. Bella didn't want to tell Zion, but she was exhausted. It was getting hard to breathe. She had to constantly remind herself not to look down. Her brain protested each step. The excitement of the adventure had finally worn off. Bella finally felt fear creep into every crevice of her body.

The wind picked up and Bella had to hold her hair back so she could see.

Distracted from her fears for a moment, she looked down. Her legs turned to jelly.

"Are you tired?" Zion asked. He looked into her eyes with concern.

"Yes! I know we're almost to the top of the tower, but I'm wiped out. I can't do this anymore."

"Let's find a place to rest."

They found a secluded section of the tower between two columns that jutted out into the walkway.

She had to find something else to focus on. "Zion, I had the craziest, uh, vision."

"Wait," Zion interrupted. He held out a hand to stop Bella from saying anything else.

A new horde of workers and wolves trotted past. The men carried buckets and bricks, and the wolves carried vicious looks with open mouths and bared fangs. The builders and the beasts.

Bella never finished explaining to Zion what she'd seen, because when the path was clear, he jumped up and pulled Bella to her feet. "We have to hurry. Come on."

"I want to go home."

Zion held her hands. "You will. Soon. I promise. For now, we need to get you to the top of the tower!"

Bella took a deep breath and exhaled. She had to fight against the fear.

They moved more quickly, watching in every direction for danger. Bella half-expected Gol to jump out at any moment to grab her or send his wolves to attack them.

After another long stretch of time climbing the

tower, Zion pointed at something above them. "Look!"

Bella followed his finger. "The top?"

"Yes!"

She was exhausted. Her legs ached. Her nerves were frayed. The smallest shadow caused anxiety. Her heart felt heavy in her chest. Instead of celebrating, Bella felt *done.* Done with the tower. Done with trying to escape wolves and wild men. Done with being away from her family.

"Bella? You okay?"

"No. I don't feel right. I thought I could make it, but something's not right."

"You can make it!"

Maybe what she was feeling was a panic attack. She heard a lot of people got them. Bella tried taking a deep breath, but she wasn't getting enough air. Each gulp brought more anxiety instead of oxygen.

"Zion, I don't feel good. I need to go back down."

"Come on, Bella. You've got this! We made it."

But she didn't *have this.*

Zion stepped to the side of the path to where a huge clay pot stood. He fished through the pot and pulled out a red beanie. "Put it on!"

But Bella didn't feel like doing anything. She was

overwhelmed with anxiety. All the stress of being in this forsaken place had finally caught up with her. She thought she was strong, but now she knew that simply wasn't the case.

"Come on, Bella! Put it on. Remember how all the other pieces of armor helped you get to this place. The helmet will help you remember who you *really* are."

Bella didn't feel like remembering. Suddenly it was like her eyes were finally opened to just how high up in the air she was. It felt like she was miles off the ground. Worse than that, the wind grew wilder, whipping the tower with stronger and stronger gusts of unrelenting force. If she didn't get down from there, Bella felt that she was accepting certain death.

She felt helpless, like she was about to be blown off the tower whether she kept walking or stayed crouched against the tower wall.

"Don't quit now!" Zion held out the beanie. "I can't put it on for you. You have to decide!"

Bella closed her eyes and imagined what it would feel like to be blown off the tower. At first, it would probably feel like a bird flying. Then—

"BELLA!"

The shout jarred her eyes open. Zion was still there

holding out the red hat. His face, normally pleasant and inviting, was crunched up and ultra-serious.

"COME ON!"

Bella shook her head. Even though they had only a few more steps to go before they reached the top, fear had finally worked its way into her brain. It overrode her rational thinking and told her that going back down and getting far away from this place was the only option to survive.

"Zion, I have to get off the tower. I don't know what I was thinking, but I have to get out of here and try to find a way home."

The workers lugged heavy bricks and set them on tar, forming a new level of the tower. They were yelling words Bella couldn't understand. A few of the men saw Bella and Zion, but they just kept up their furious pace of setting the bricks to make the tower go even higher.

Bella didn't know where heaven began, but they were so high up in the air it had to be close.

Without another thought, she grabbed the hat from Zion. It felt like energy was flowing back and forth over the fabric. *Just like the breastplate.* Just having the hat in her hand seemed to erase some of the negative feelings that had filled her mind.

God is not leaving me. He never leaves His children!

Bella slipped on the hat.

I am God's daughter. I am not a slave to the world. I do not have to be afraid of this overwhelming tower.

She noticed a smile on Zion's face. "I'm proud of you, Bella!"

God is my Abba, my Daddy. He is not some stranger, far away and uncaring. My heart is filled by His endless love.

Her whole body felt different. She felt brave.

Yes, my heart needs Your love, Jesus. Thank You, Holy Spirit, for reminding me of this.

Bella felt strong and prayed that her fear would be erased.

God loves me so much that He is constantly guiding me.

Bella had the feeling that God was using the dangers on the tower for something greater.

It was time to finish what she started. It was time to confront the workers and ask them to stop building.

"I'm Bella Rhodes." Although the builders kept working, some slowed and looked at her. "Please stop building this tower."

The workers who noticed her chuckled, like she had asked them to eat lizards.

"This tower is not the answer. Obeying God is. He

wants you to go and spread out over all the land."

By some miracle, all the workers stopped what they were doing and faced Bella. Were they actually going to listen to her?

A handful of seconds passed. The workers just stood there looking at her.

That's when Bella sensed someone standing behind her.

"Finish the tower!" She knew the voice and who it belonged to.

Bella turned and saw a terrible sight. It was Gol.

The evil one carried a huge sword.

"Finish the tower, while I finish the girl!"

Gol brought down the sword.

CHAPTER FOURTEEN

The wind was so strong Bella couldn't keep her eyes open for more than a few seconds at a time. But for the short time they were open, she saw the metal blade come down over her.

She tried to move out of the way, but it happened so fast. . . She threw her hands up in self-defense and felt the heavy blade smash into. . .her shield?

Yes, it was the shield that Zion had given her. It was right there now, between her outstretched hands. A strong defense against her enemy's blade.

It came again, Gol's sword, like a flash of lightning. This time from the left. . .

And again, Bella moved the shield to intercept the blow.

She looked around for Zion, but she couldn't find her friend.

"YOU DON'T BELONG HERE!"

Gol's scream seemed to swirl around in the wind that was coming faster now. His words moved around Bella like an animal circling its prey.

Gol lunged toward Bella, causing her to jump back. She lost her footing and fell down. She was trapped. The builders kept building like the life of a young girl wasn't being threatened right in front of them by a sword-wielding maniac.

Gol picked her up and shoved her toward the tower. Her head hit the wall and she fell again, flat on her back, but the helmet she was wearing protected her.

Thank You, God!

"Bella!" Zion's voice came to her through the craziness. She couldn't take her eyes off Gol. She hoped her friend had a plan, or this whole thing was going to end in disaster.

"Now I will finish you!" Gol brought the sword down a third time.

Bella's feet vibrated. *The shoes!*

She raised them up, and the enemy's blade crashed into the cleats. Bella's body vibrated from the blow.

She rolled over to stand and get out of the way. The blade came down again and nicked her right arm. It felt

91

like an ant bite. Blood pooled on her skin.

Again, Bella shuffled to her left to avoid another blow from Gol's blade.

And again, the blade came down...

Bella jumped back, close to the edge...

The sword struck her left shoulder but did not cut her. The breastplate! The shirt buzzed with protective energy.

Bella undid her belt and threw it around Gol's feet. Zion jumped over to help, and both of them yanked the rope hard. They pulled Gol off his feet.

Not to be undone by two kids, the wicked man got up and went after Zion. He swung the sword at him. Zion spun away and missed getting impaled by inches. He bent over to pick something up, but Bella couldn't see what it was.

Gol rushed Zion and tackled him to the ground. Bella ran over to help.

"I gave you plenty of warnings. You are foolish children who don't know when to quit." Gol shoved Zion to the edge of the path. The workers kept building. Bella tried to think of a plan.

"Bella!" Zion pointed at the ground by his feet.

She looked but couldn't see what he was pointing to.

"What is it, Zion?"

He didn't answer. Gol was backing Zion up to the edge of tower path.

"Zion!"

Her friend kept pointing.

Bella finally saw it. A sword! Not the one Gol had been using. This one was small. Kid size.

Gol turned and saw it too.

Zion got up, long enough to distract Gol and give Bella time to grab the weapon.

Bella got to the sword before Gol had a chance to. She grabbed it and felt more energy flow through her hands and arms. It made her feel powerful.

The builders kept building, ignoring the conflict behind them.

"I don't care how many weapons you have. A little girl is not going to stop me!" Gol turned and lunged at Zion. Zion moved back but lost his footing.

"Zion!"

Bella couldn't believe what happened. One minute her friend was on the tower path, the next he'd slipped over the edge. She could see his hands gripping the walkway, trying to hold on.

Gol inched his way to the edge. He turned to watch Bella.

"I told you to go home. You didn't listen. Now look what you did."

"Help him up!" Bella looked for a way to get to Zion. One of Zion's hands lost its grip. "Help him!"

Then the other hand let go.

"NO!"

Bella lifted her sword and charged Gol. The adrenaline flowed through her body and she swung the sword at the bad man like she was a major league homerun slugger.

Gol used his sword to block Bella's blow, but her angle and speed was so on point that his sword fell out of his hand. Bella swung again. Gol ducked out of the way.

Then her worst fear came true. The wolves returned with a vengeance. Six of the hideous creatures arrived to protect their master. They blocked her way back down the tower. There was no way out.

"To show you I'm not as bad as you think," Gol said, "I will let you put your sword down and join me."

"Never!" Bella thought of Zion. She couldn't save him. She wasn't going to let Gol beat her.

Gol closed his eyes. "As you wish. Lyaar, kill her!"

CHAPTER FIFTEEN

The massive tower was now her prison. Its heavy stone walls rose up around her, making any chance of escape impossible. Still, she had run as fast as her young legs could move, hoping to find a way to stop the evil army from reaching heaven. She had put up a good fight to get this far, but it wasn't good enough. She had run straight into a dead end, and the hideous wolf blocked her only way out. The finish line of life was just ahead, covered in mangy fur and sharp fangs. Death was going to greet Bella through the teeth of a wolf.

She was so high up in the air it felt like she was standing at the entrance to heaven. The spiral walkway she had used to ascend the tower with Zion was now empty. Where had all the people gone? Bella hated heights, but to survive the dreaded monster, she had to get over it. The evil one named Gol had already pushed her friend over the edge. . .

She was next.

Her eyes locked on to the honey-colored wolf eyes that were locked on her. She could see evil swirling in those yellow orbs like a sulfurous potion brewed in cauldrons of darkest night. The predator inched closer. Five more evil hounds ran up and took their positions behind the alpha. All six were about to tear Bella into a pile of human confetti.

The animals started their chorus of deep, slow growls.

All she could do was stand her ground.

And pray.

Dear God, help me!

The wolf lunged at Bella. She used the sword to block the attack. Part of her weapon sliced Lyaar's front legs. The animal yelped and scurried to the back of the pack. The remaining five wolves, in unison, pounced at Bella. All she could do was spin in a tight circle, holding her sword out.

Like a human blender, the blade did its job, keeping the animals from attacking her.

Climbing over his cringing animals, Gol attacked Bella.

An explosion of light ripped across the sky above

them. Thunder rattled the tower in reply.

Before he could raise his sword, she executed a jumping front kick, planting the cleats of her right shoe straight into the middle of Gol's chest. He dropped the sword and grabbed his heart. A red splotch appeared on Gol's robe. It spread like wildfire through a dry forest of brittle trees.

Bella snatched up his sword and held both blades as she took a guarding stance. Gol looked at her in disbelief. Bella jumped and kicked him again, cleats connecting with the backs of his folded hands.

Blood dripped and spread.

In a flash, Bella brought both blades down, but Gol had enough sense to jump back. She saw how close to the edge he was, so she stuck the swords out in front of her and lunged.

Her roar was an intimidating scream.

Another blast of light from heaven lit up the tower's precipice.

Before the points of Bella's swords reached him, the bolt of lightning found its mark and slammed into Gol's chest.

Bella stopped short as she witnessed the man's body get thrown backward. . .

. . .over the tower's edge.

She watched the evil figure fall like a speeding roller coaster down the first big hill.

All the way. . .

. . .down. . .

. . .to the plain. . .

. . .far. . .

. . .far. . .

. . .below.

Bella summoned strength to ward off the army of wolves that had made their way to the top of Babel. But once their master disappeared, the horde immediately turned and ran away down the tower path. It was as if Gol's demise freed them from their bond of service.

Bella couldn't believe it. Gol was gone, but so was Zion!

As she made her way back down the tower path, Bella heard heavy thunder rumble. It felt like the ground shook with each boom. Then she heard a loud voice say, *"Let us confuse the people with different languages. Then they won't be able to understand each other."*

Bella couldn't believe it. She knew the Bible story well. God had said those words!

How was this happening?

She kept going, following the path down from the top, still not believing that her friend was gone. All the people she passed were yelling at each other. It looked and sounded to Bella like no one could understand what the other was saying.

Everyone had a look of sheer panic painted on their faces. They kept yelling and tugging on each other. They made hand motions to try to communicate their needs. Bella kept going, but the loss she felt for Zion was overwhelming. Tears were running down her cheeks. She couldn't believe she would never see him again.

She was rounding a part of the tower that jutted out into the path when she saw someone sitting up against the tower, face pressed against his knees. As she passed by him, she heard her name. "Bella?"

"Zion?" She turned. It was Zion! "How. . .how did you—?"

"I'm not dead. When I fell, I landed on some wolves. The wicked creatures broke my fall."

Bella laughed.

"What's so funny?"

"I know what you mean!"

Zion looked confused. "When have you ever fallen off the side of a tower?"

"No, not that! I'm laughing because I understand the words coming out of your mouth."

Zion still didn't get it.

"Zion, look around. God made these people speak in different languages. Now they can't understand what each other is saying. They're going nuts. Running to get off the tower and find someone who can understand."

"Oh, that's wild. I can understand you too!"

"Are you okay to stand up?" Bella put out a hand to help her friend.

"I think so." Zion grabbed Bella's hand and stood.

They made their way down the tower path, cutting through groups of people who were yelling and shouting. No one had any idea what had happened. One minute they were talking to their friends and the next minute they couldn't understand each other.

"Bella, here's the plan before something else happens and we can't understand each other. I have a couple of friends not too far from here. We'll go meet up with them and figure things out."

"Let's go!"

Bella and Zion made their way down the long tower path. They ran through clusters of people who were all freaking out.

It was getting dark by the time they made it half-way down the tower. Bella couldn't believe that all the wolves had vanished. The farther down they went, the more Babel looked like a ghost town. Bella could only guess that the people were all running far away from the tower, hoping to find other humans who spoke the same language.

"Zion, how far away are your friends?"

"Mark and Josephine are very close."

Bella walked next to her friend in silence, over-whelmed by the mass hysteria that had taken over the people who lived and worked on the tower.

She was getting very tired. Her legs and eyes felt heavy.

"Zion, can we rest?"

"Sure. I told my friends that if they didn't see us by nightfall to come look for us."

"Sorry, it's just hard 'cause I'm getting really sleepy."

"Don't worry. You'll get all the rest you need."

"Thanks for taking care of me."

Bella sat down against the tower wall and closed her eyes. She was exhausted. She yawned.

"You're welcome." Zion sat down next to her.

Bella drifted off into a fitful slumber, wracked by

dreams of fighting evil. Somewhere in the middle of the nightmares, she yelled.

Her time had come. . .

CHAPTER SIXTEEN

. . .to go home.

"Are you okay, Bel? You look like you've seen a ghost!"

Bella blinked. She looked around and saw that the tower had glass windows and steel beams. Carpet, and people that dressed like she did.

"Eva, I'm okay."

"You sure?"

"Yes." Bella knew Eva wouldn't understand. Her parents wouldn't buy it either.

"Sweetheart, what happened?" Her dad sounded super concerned.

"I don't know. I think I felt light-headed and then my legs forgot how to hold me up."

"Okay, we're going get you out of here and back to the hotel."

While the Rhodes family waited for the elevator, a

girl Bella's age stared at her. Bella ignored her.

"You're Bella, right? I'm Zee. I love writing. Your videos have inspired me to finish my first story!"

It was hard for Bella to concentrate. Her brain was flooded with memories of Babel. Where did it go? Where was Zion? Could she go back again?

"What's your name?"

"Well, it's Zeeamara, but I go by Zee."

Bella heard the girl but couldn't believe it.

Zee.

Like Zion.

I miss you, friend.

"Hi, Zee. Thanks for telling me that. I'm really glad I got to meet you."

Bella noticed the girl was wearing a San Diego Padres ball cap with the navy interlocking SD embroidered on it.

"You're not from San Diego, are you?" Bella asked.

"Yes, I am!"

"I saw your Padres cap and wondered."

"I would guess that you don't live in Chicago. I don't think people who live here visit the top of Willis Tower often." Zee looked at Bella like they were old friends who hadn't seen each other in years.

"We live in San Diego too!" Bella was excited.

They exchanged phone numbers and promised to keep in touch.

The Rhodes family walked outside, back into the chilly Chicago afternoon. Bella stopped and looked up at Willis Tower climbing toward heaven. It seemed impossible to think that just moments ago, she had climbed Babel. Here, back in the *now,* she felt different. More alive. God had shown up big time and protected her when she couldn't protect herself.

God helped her stand up for what was right.

Bella took a deep breath. She followed her parents and sister down the street. Cold air whipped around her face and hair just like it had on the Tower of Babel.

She watched her breath blow away like smoky mist on the frigid air. As it disappeared, she couldn't help but think of how quickly the Bible adventure at Shinar had vanished.

"Are you okay, honey?" It was her mom this time. "You seem quiet."

Bella was thinking about her YouTube channel. She didn't feel so anxious to check it as she did before. At least not for the same reason she had before this whole experience. She knew she'd made it her idol. The more subscribers she had, the more worthy she felt. It felt really good to have people acknowledge her.

But God just acknowledged her in a massive way!

Her heart had changed. She wanted His approval.

Bella knew right then what she had to do. She had to use her online presence to make God famous.

"I'm great!"

Bella grabbed one of her mom's hands and one of Eva's. She led them in skipping down the sidewalk.

"You're weird!" Eva shouted.

"Thank you!"

It felt so good to be back with her family. Back to normal. Except it wasn't normal, because the tower experience had opened her eyes to the love and power of God.

Bella had a random thought. She remembered that Zee mentioned finishing her story. She was curious. Bella pulled up Zee's number and typed a quick text.

WHAT'S UR STORY ABOUT?

Bella closed her eyes and said a quick prayer. *Thank You, Lord, for being with me. Thank You for loving me.*

She didn't know how all of it happened, but Bella was

glad to have a new friend in Zee. God was so creative. Bella couldn't wait to see what came next.

KIDS WHO GO BACK 2 BIBLE TIMES!

Bella almost dropped her phone. How could this be?

ZEE, UR STORY SOUNDS GREAT. I'D LUV 2 READ IT WHEN WE GET HOME.

"Stop looking at your phone," Bella's mom said. "We're trying to be a family who interacts with each other on vacation."

U SPELL MY NAME XI. LOL. THX 4 READING MY STORY.

"Okay, let me tell Xi bye."

TTYL

A cold gust of wind blew over Bella and made her shiver. She started to put her phone in her pocket when her phone dinged. Xi was fast.

MY 1ST CHARACTER CLIMBS THE TOWER OF BABEL. LATER.

Bella spun around to see if Xi was still there, but she had disappeared into the crowd.

EPILOGUE

The encounter he had just witnessed was all he needed to keep going.

Watching Konrad Lynch personally escort Ka'nah away from the Oak Bay property was a sign that the end was coming and coming soon. The guard didn't follow directions, and now he had finally lost his leadership position.

He stared a bit longer at the *ALIAS* website. The tracking portal confirmed that *Team Zion* was assembled. Also, *Team Moriah* was initiated with the recruitment of Bella Rhodes. Her visit to Shinar had alerted the watchers that a second group was being gathered.

He didn't know how many teams there would be. He only knew that now that the second team was started, the Enemy's plan would accelerate.

Daemon closed his laptop and smiled. Because of his patience and attention to detail, he was now in charge of the watchers and of disrupting any future teams to be created.

There was so much work left to do. But the best part of his new position was the gathering of soldiers for the Master's army.

The battle was getting closer. He couldn't wait.

But he had to be patient.

Patience.

Yes, that's what he had to have. That's what had gotten him this far.

Because escaping the fire and getting back to heaven was going to be worth the wait.

Forever was a very long time and now, because of his hard work and waiting, it was going to be awesome.

DON'T MISS THESE EPIC ADVENTURES IN THE IMAGINE SERIES!

Imagine. . .The Great Flood

The last thing ten-year-old Corey remembers (before the world as he knew it disappeared) was the searing pain in his head after falling while chasing his dog, Molly, into the woods. What happens next can't be explained as Corey wakes up and finds himself face-to-face with not one but *two* lions!

Paperback / 978-1-68322-129-6 / $5.99

Imagine. . .The Ten Plagues

The last thing fourth-grader Kai Wells remembers (before the world as she knew it disappeared) is being surrounded by bullies on her walk home from school. What happens next can't be explained as Kai finds herself on the run for her life in ancient Egypt!

Paperback / 978-1-68322-380-1 / $5.99

Imagine. . . The Fall of Jericho

The last thing fifth-grader Jake Henry remembers (before the world as he knew it disappeared) is napping at summer camp. What happens next can't be explained as Jake finds himself surrounded by massive stone walls that rise up all around him—in ancient Jericho!

Paperback / 978-1-68322-714-4 / $5.99

Imagine. . . The Giant's Fall

The last thing fourth-grader Wren Evans remembers (before the world as she knew it disappeared) is getting off the school bus to discover her house engulfed in flames. What happens next can't be explained as Wren finds herself in a beautiful valley with a shepherd named David—in ancient Israel!

Paperback / 978-1-68322-944-5 / $5.99